Little Owl's Egg

For all Owls: Big, Small, or Eggs.
This one's for you with love —D. G.

For Edward and Isobel —A. B.

First published in Great Britain in October 2016 by Bloomsbury Publishing Plc
Published in the United States of America in November 2017
by Bloomsbury Children's Books
www.bloomsbury.com

Bloomsbury is a registered trademark of Bloomsbury Publishing Plc

For information about permission to reproduce selections from this book, write to
Permissions, Bloomsbury Children's Books, 1385 Broadway, New York, New York 10018
Bloomsbury books may be purchased for business or promotional use. For information on bulk purchases
please contact Macmillan Corporate and Premium Sales Department at specialmarkets@macmillan.com

Library of Congress Cataloging-in-Publication Data
available upon request
ISBN 978-1-68119-324-3 (hardcover)

Art created with acrylic paint and colored pencil
Typeset in Mrs Eaves and Duper Pro
Book design by Kristina Coates
Printed in China by Leo Paper Products, Heshan, Guangdong
2 4 6 8 10 9 7 5 3 1

All papers used by Bloomsbury Publishing, Inc., are natural, recyclable products
made from wood grown in well-managed forests. The manufacturing processes
conform to the environmental regulations of the country of origin.

Little Owl's Egg

Debi Gliori

illustrated by
Alison Brown

BLOOMSBURY

NEW YORK   LONDON   OXFORD   NEW DELHI   SYDNEY

Little Owl's mommy had some very exciting news. She had laid a beautiful egg.

"Guess what?" said Little Owl's mommy. "We're having a new baby owl."

"NO," said Little Owl.

"NO,

NO,

NO!"

"No?" said Mommy.

"NO," said Little Owl.
"I'm your baby owl. You
don't need a new one."

Mommy Owl blinked.
"Silly me," she said. "You're right.
Besides, this egg is far too quiet
to be a baby owl . . .

. . . Perhaps it's a baby worm.
They're so silent and undemanding.
Just a bowl of dirt from time to time . . .
Wouldn't that be lovely?"

Not a wiggly worm.

EWWWWW."

Mommy Owl smiled.
"No," she said. "You're right.
It doesn't wiggle. Perhaps
it's a pretend egg, made
of chocolate . . .

. . . Wouldn't that be good?"

"No." Little Owl sighed.
"Chocolate eggs are no fun.
They don't know how to play.
And they melt if you hug them."

Mommy Owl prodded the egg.
"You're right, Little Owl. This egg is
far too cold to be made of chocolate.
Poor egg. Feel it—it's freezing.

I wonder if we're having a
baby penguin. Goodness!
We'd better go and catch
some fish for its dinner."

"NO!"

Little Owl squeaked.

"Not a

Mommy Owl patted the egg. "What a silly mommy—penguin eggs are warm. It's crocodile eggs that are chilly. That's it. We're having a baby crocodile. I wonder what they eat?"

Little Owl's eyes grew wide.

"N-n-n-no," he whispered, "n-n-not a crocodile."

"Probably not," whispered Mommy.
"Besides, it's a huge egg. Far too
big to be a crocodile.
Perhaps it's an . . ."

"**ELEPHANT!**" yelled Little Owl. "That would be amazing. We could have the best water fights . . ."

"No," said Mommy.
"NO, NO, NO! Think of our nest.
That would be a catastrophe."

"No. You're right," said Little Owl.
"Besides, elephants can't fly.
But dragons can. Ooooh.
I hope it's a **dragon egg**."

"Oh, *goodness*,"
squeaked Mommy.
"NO, NO, NO!"

"But it is a very splendid
egg," said Little Owl.
"It must have something
very special inside . . .

. . . Perhaps it's a baby

Princess Wormy Choco-Penguin Crocophant Dragowl.

Hmmm. I've heard that they eat only very special food. Eighty-legged snort beans. Green-gloopy gargle taters . . ."

"Sounds awful."
Mommy groaned.

"You know," continued Little Owl, "a little owl just like me would be much more fun than a baby Princess Wormy Choco-Penguin Crocophant Dragowl."

"Yes," said Mommy. "We'd love a baby owl much more than a baby anything else."

Little Owl put his wings around the egg and gave it a hug. Inside, a tiny heart beat steadily.

Thud

Thud

Thud

"When will our egg be ready?" said Little Owl.

"Soon," said Mommy.

"If it's a new Little Owl, then I'll be
a new Big Owl," said Little Owl.

"Yes," said Mommy. "You'll be my new
Big Owl, and I'll love you always."

"Always?" said Little Owl.

"Always," said Mommy.